SLOW DOWN, TUMBLEWEED!

For Willa and Luther,
May you always feel free to roam, and to enjoy the beauty that is right in front of you.
—HI

To Meryl,
Who I'm incredibly lucky to experience life with.
—RS

Sounds True
Boulder, CO 80306

Text © 2021 Haven Iverson
Illustrations © 2021 Rob Sayegh Jr.

Published 2021

Book & cover design by Ranée Kahler
Cover illustration by Rob Sayegh Jr.

Printed in South Korea

LCCN 2021936245

10 9 8 7 6 5 4 3 2 1

SLOW DOWN, TUMBLEWEED!

Haven Iverson

Illustrated by Rob Sayegh Jr.

sounds true
BOULDER, COLORADO

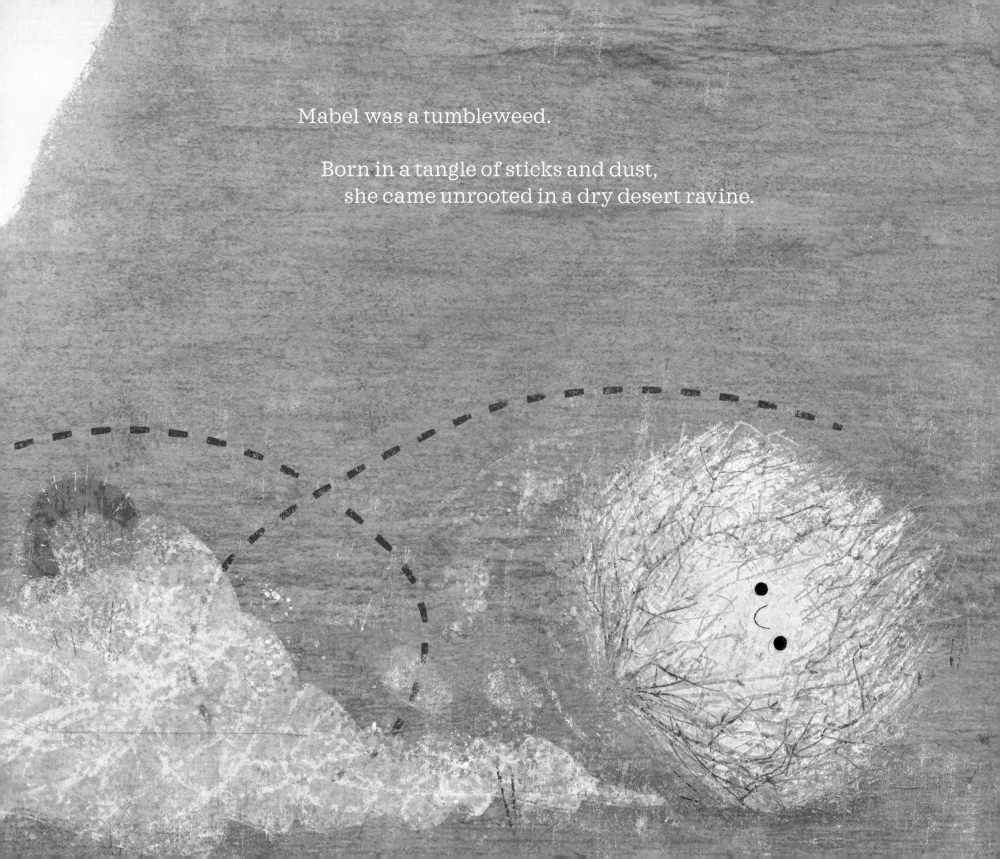

Mabel was a tumbleweed.

Born in a tangle of sticks and dust,
she came unrooted in a dry desert ravine.

From the moment she rolled out from her thicket of weeds, she tumbled.

She **RAMBLED** and **RUMBLED**

and rode the wind.

She screamed across highways.
Skidded through desert flats.

Always a trail of dirt at her backside.

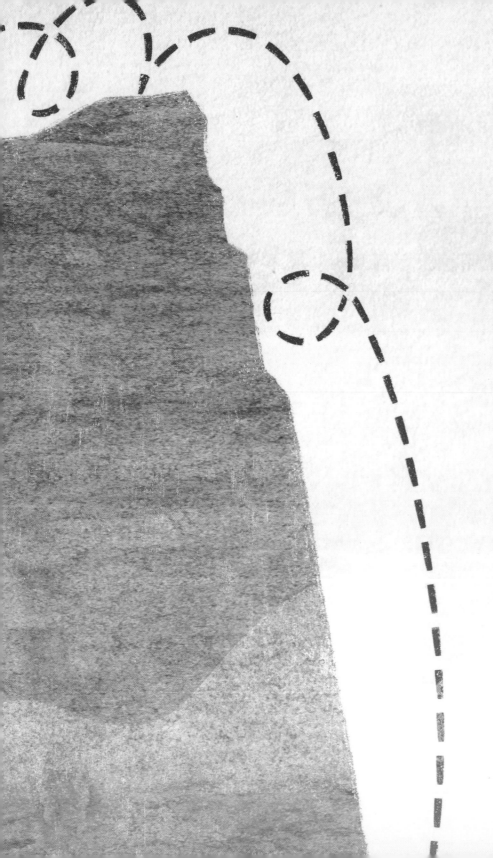

Life was amazing!
And to see it all,
experience it all,
discover it all,
you had to

GO ...

GO ...

GO!

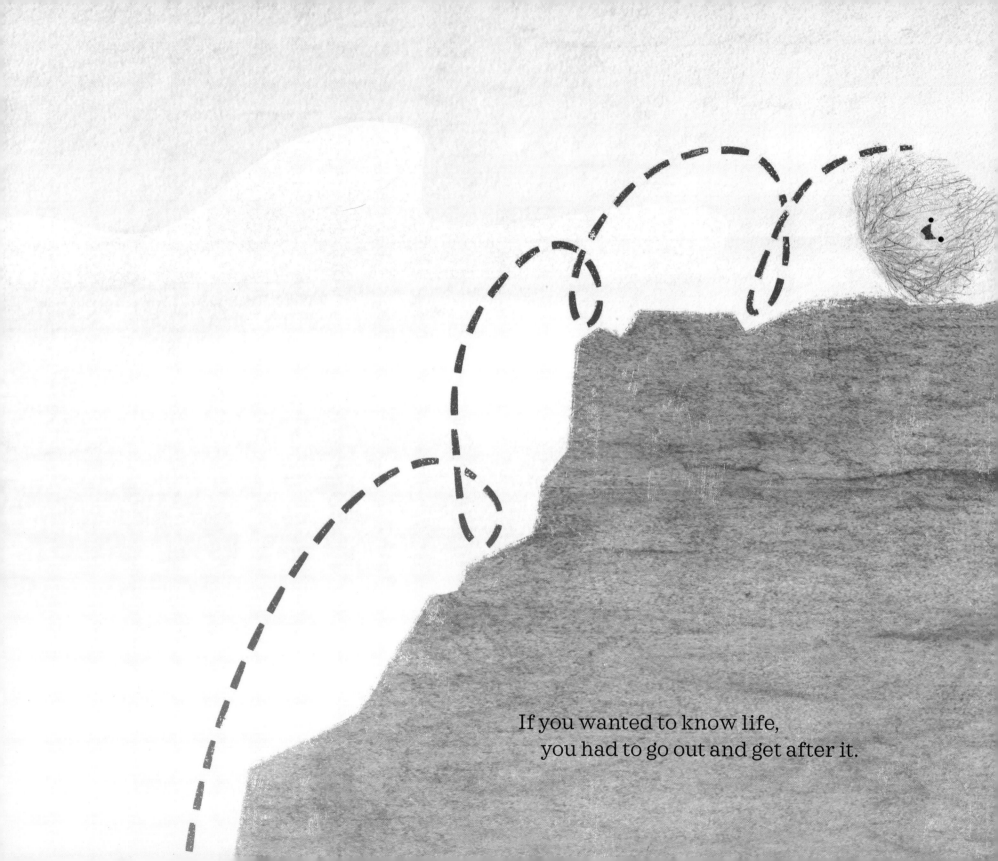

If you wanted to know life,
you had to go out and get after it.

Cars honked.
Bobcats chased.

HONK! HONK!

And varmints of every shape and size
screeched to a halt as she happily hooted by.

By the time she was five, she'd tumbled forty miles to Lubbock and back.

By the time she was six, she visited at least a dozen new places a day.

She even danced the night
currents in her sleep.
Sure, she was a weed,
but she was free.

Passing over all the other weeds,
   rooted in the ground,
      she felt sorry for them.
How dull their lives must be, unable to **ROAM AND ROLL.**

Lifeless, she thought, as she hurled herself around
   bales of hay and curly top knotweed.

Boring, she determined, as she tossed over a tractor,
   stinknet and toadflax weeds motionless on the horizon.

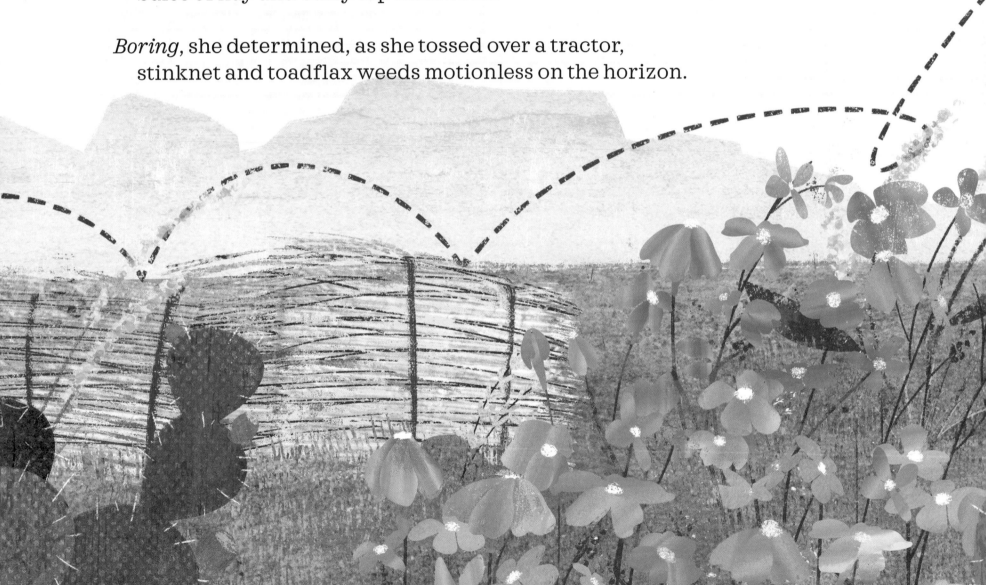

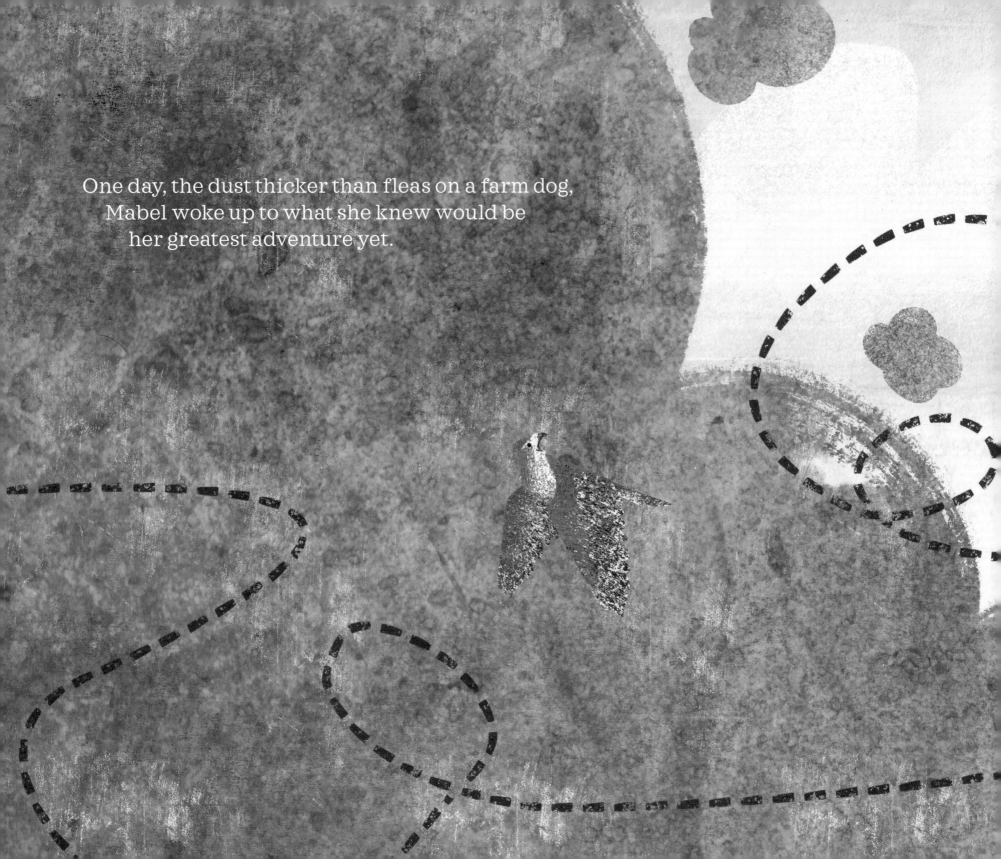

One day, the dust thicker than fleas on a farm dog,
Mabel woke up to what she knew would be
her greatest adventure yet.

The wind was grand.

She would swing higher than ever before.
Maybe even travel as far as the state line.

As she unfurled herself to the gusts, she
whooped and whirled, twisted and twirled.
"LIFE!" SHE BALLYHOOED.

By high noon she was on the upside of the current, spiraling north.
An hour later, she was a blur, a whirly wheel of sticks and twigs.

The armadillos were in awe. The coyotes, transfixed.

But minutes later, as she
    rambled east,
a wind swept west flinging
    her backward,
    past an old hog and hen
taking a dust bath . . .

and against a barn and a fence, where
she came to a complete standstill.

She waited for a wind, a gust, even the slightest flurry, to push her along, but it did not come.

She tugged, she heaved.
But she did not budge.
SHE WAS STUCK.
Like a weed in the ground.

Mabel's heart grew heavy.
  Stillness was scary!
Life would become dull, boring, lifeless.

As day turned to night, tears began to drip
  down her twigs.

Moonlight cast shadows of tall,
fancy cacti on the barn wall beside her,
but her eyes were too fogged
with tears to notice.

A handsome badger stopped
to see if she was okay,
but she missed it entirely,
her sobs were so deep and loud.

For hours, she cried, then tugged,
tugged, then cried, twisting her tangled body to get free.

But eventually she grew too tired to keep trying.

So, as the sun came up, she just ... **SAT THERE.**

Mabel watched the light of the morning sun
    waltz across the tall grass in the distance.

Clouds stretched across the sky and
    she saw formations she'd never seen.
She heard a wind chime, music more
    lovely than she'd ever known.

And when a she-cow paused nearby,
    Mabel marveled at her eyelashes,
    long and lush and thick as prairie grass.

MABEL WAS TRANSFIXED.

So much life and beauty delivered
directly to her as she sat.

Eventually, as things go, the perfect gust
ambled along, and Mabel broke free.
SHE ROLLED AND RAMBLED.

But she'd only gone a few yards before
she stopped in the open light.

There, Mabel settled into the quiet of her mind,
so she could find sweet stillness once again.
Just sitting there, there was so much to see.
So much to experience.
So much to discover.
So much life, tumbling out
right before her very eyes.

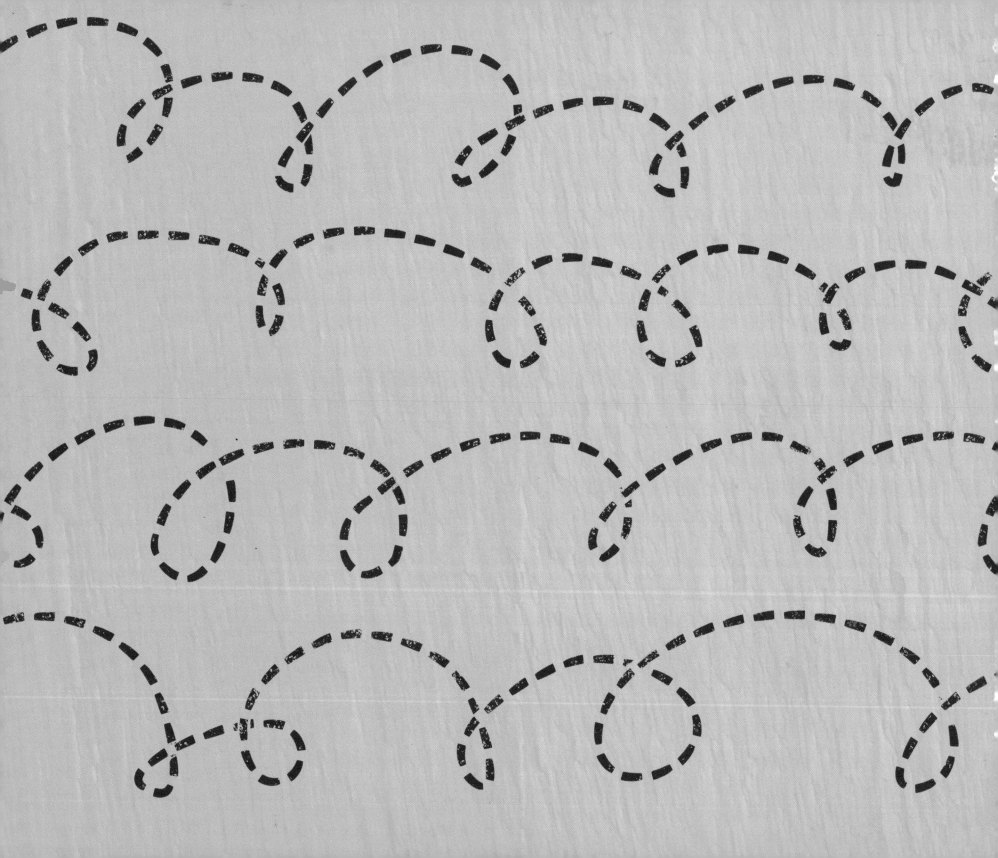